SPIRIT OF HOPE

To my mother and father

For David Allsop,
my thoughts and my thanks

This edition published in the United States of America in 1996
by MONDO Publishing
First published in Australia in 1993 by Thomas C. Lothian Pty Ltd

For information contact:
MONDO Publishing
One Plaza Road
Greenvale, New York 11548

Printed in Hong Kong
First Mondo printing, July 1996
96 97 98 99 00 01   9 8 7 6 5 4 3 2 1

Library of Congress Cataloging-in-Publication Data
Graham, Bob, 1942-
    Spirit of Hope / Bob Graham.
       p.   cm.
    Summary: When the Fairweather family almost gives up hope
of finding a place to live, the youngest child gives them an idea for
a great location.
    ISBN 1-57255-202-6 (hc). — ISBN 1-57255-201-8 (pb)
[1. Hope—Fiction. 2. Moving, Household—Fiction. 3. Family
life—Fiction.] I. Title.
PZ7.G751667Sp   1996
[E]—dc20
                                            96-6352
                                             CIP
                                             AC

SPIRIT OF HOPE

BOB GRAHAM

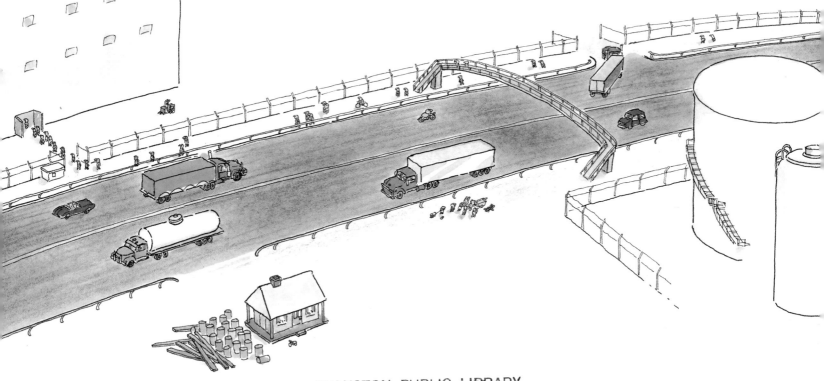

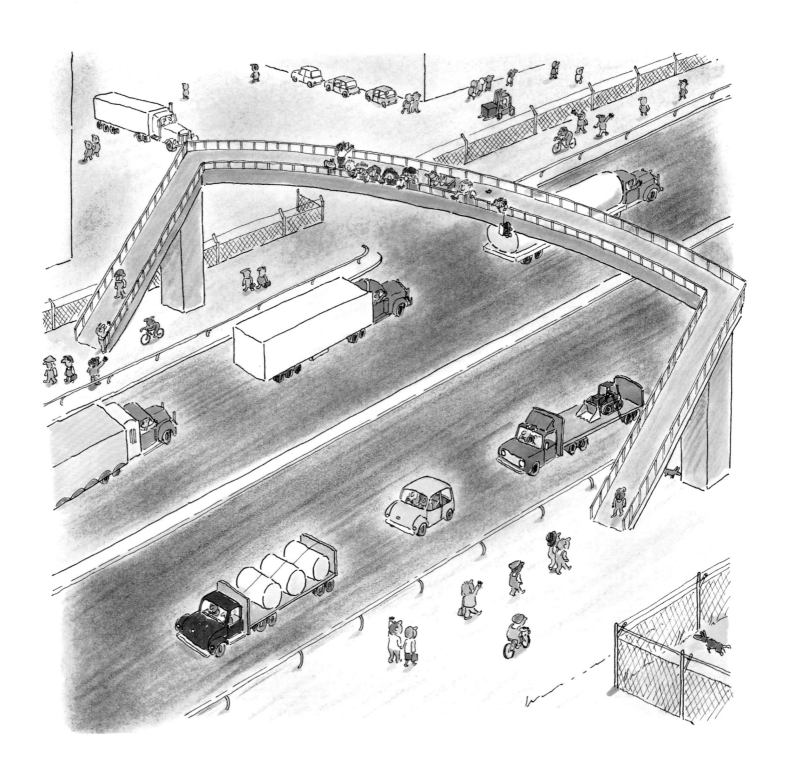

Six days a week, the Fairweathers crossed the bridge. They waved to the passing trucks and the drivers waved back. Everyone knew the Fairweathers, and the Fairweathers knew everyone.

Six days a week, the Fairweathers said good-bye to Dad at the factory gate, his lunch tucked under his arm in a brown paper bag.

Six nights a week, Dad returned from work. The welcome he received was second to none.
Each night he made the journey to the bathroom on his hands and knees.

Lilly sat up front, then Cecily and Micky, Duggy and
Sammy, Jock the dog, Bumper and Thumper, and
Trevor the tortoise.

And last of all there was Mary,
the youngest Fairweather.

Dad washed off the oil from the factory.
He scrubbed his nails, ten little black crescent moons
in a sea of foam. And he sang, "The Owl and the
Pussycat went to sea in a beautiful pea green boat . . ."

Then Mom sang, "Little Mary Fairweather dancing in the snow. Wiggle-wiggle-wiggle. Go, go, go."

And Dad did his bird calls. "Hopeless," yelled Micky. "Let's be a ship at sea," they called.

A chair was put on the kitchen table.
"Who's the Captain tonight?" called Lilly.
"Sammy can be Captain," Mom replied.
"Say it, Dad, *say it!*" they yelled.

"Full steam ahead," said Dad. "Let's imagine our house
is a ship at sea, chugging along in the darkness. Listen to
the engines. Pom-da-pom-da-pom."
Sammy sat up in the chair with the Captain's hat on and
steered the house to faraway and exotic places.

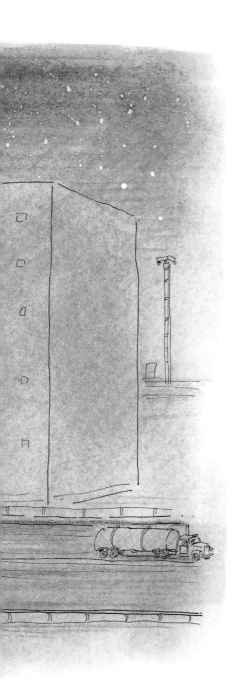

Then Lilly and Cecily, Micky and Duggy,
Sammy and Mary would climb into bed
and go to sleep with the sound of the
big trucks rolling by in the night.

The seventh day was picnic day on the docks, with plum jam sandwiches, root beer, and fruit cake. They heard the cries of the gulls and the slap of water on the hulls of the ships.

One day, they saw sailors from a faraway port.
"Join us for our picnic," called Dad. "What is the name
of your ship?"
"Spirit of Hope," the sailors shouted.

As the Fairweathers returned home from their picnic, it seemed that their house was an island where the sun always shone.

But that evening, everything changed. There was a knock at the door.

"Are you the Fairweathers?" asked one of the men.
"Yes," replied Dad. "Come in."
"No, thank you," said the man. "We have come to
inform you that you must move."
Twelve faces stared at him.
"And soon," he added.

"Why must me move?" Lilly asked.

"To make way for a factory," Dad replied.

"A factory? Where?" Cecily asked.

"Here," said Mom, pointing to the floor.

"What for?" Micky asked.

"For matchsticks," replied Dad.

"A factory to make matchsticks," Mom repeated.

"And what will happen to our dear little house?"

There was silence.

"Matchsticks," Dad replied, and put his head
in his hands.

That night, there were no Captains steering the ship
from the kitchen table.
A gloomy silence hung over the Fairweather house.

"We must not despair," said Mom. "We must keep up
a spirit of hope."

"No matter what happens, at least we are together.
Tomorrow we shall look for a new house."

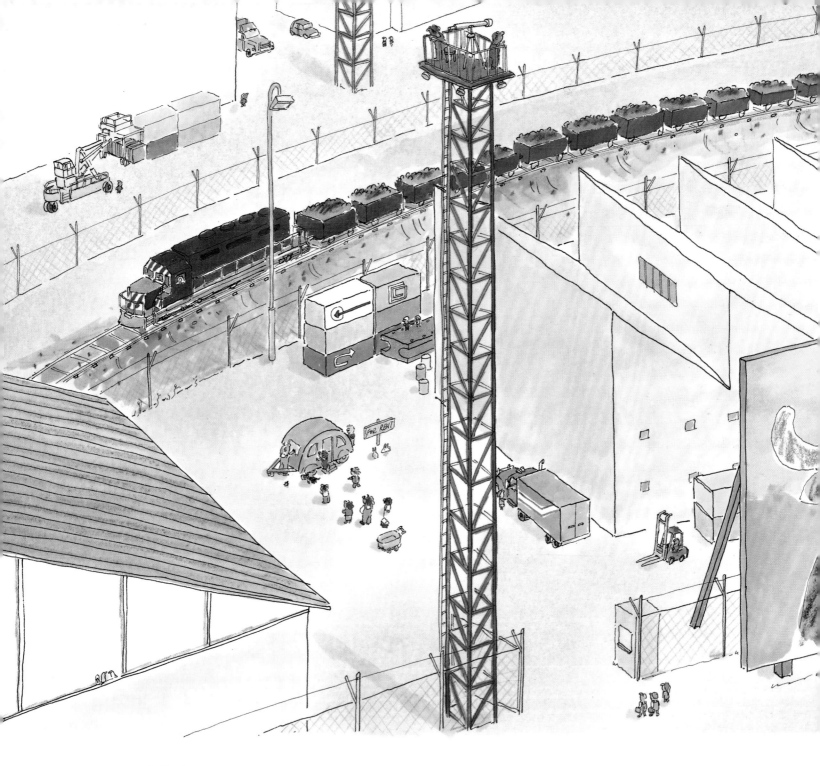

All the next week the Fairweathers searched with hope. Their
friends all searched, too. All they found were warehouses,
factories, storage lots, and one small trailer out near the railway.
"Too small," said Dad.
"No grass for the rabbits," said Cecily.

"We'll try again next week," said Mom.
Mary said nothing.

The following week, the Fairweathers searched in despair
until they could search no more.
"I feel," said Dad, "that we are adrift on a sea of trouble."

"Well, *I* feel," said Mom, looking at Mary, "that the answer to our troubles is closer than we thought. Quick, Mary, we have no time to lose."

"What are we going to do?" asked the children.
"No time to explain," replied Mom.
Mary's house bumped along all the way home.

"It must be something to do with Mary," said Lilly.
"No, it's *nothing* to do with Mary," said Cecily.
"Hurry," called Mom. "Bring those planks over here."

"Yes, it *is* Mary," said Micky.
"And her toy house," added Duggy.

"Roll those drums over here.
Hurry!" cried Mom.

The excavator clawed its way to the corner of their house.
"We're too late," shouted Dad. "All is lost."
"We need our friends," yelled Mom.
"Help!" cried the Fairweathers.

And the Fairweathers' friends came from everywhere.

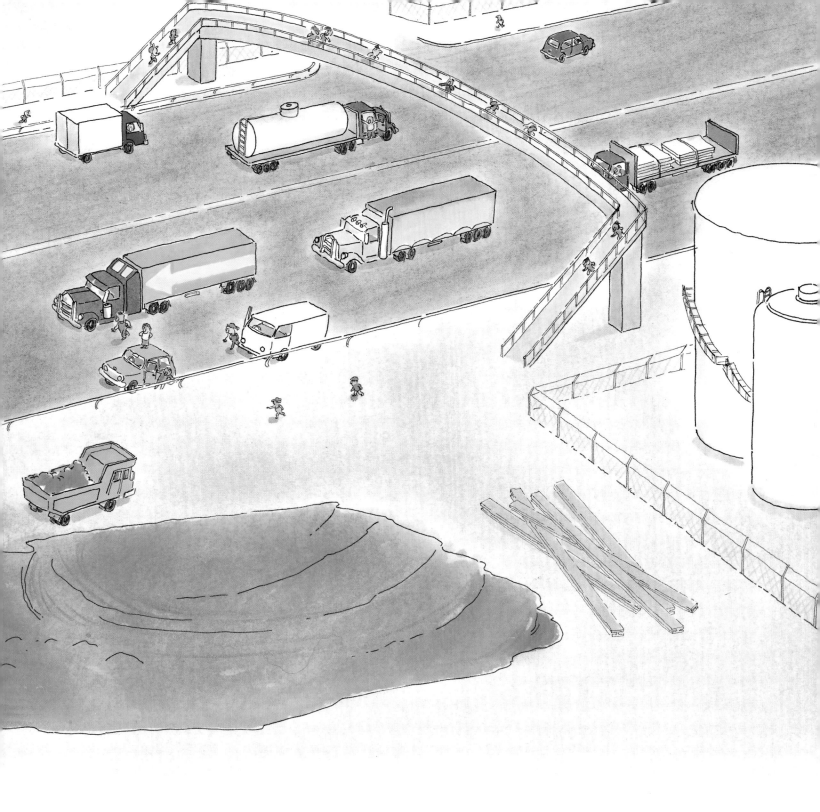

Mary Fairweather watched everything, her toy house
dangling from its string.

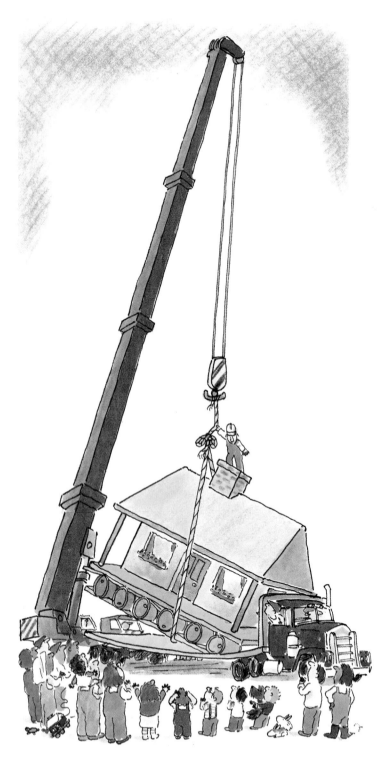

With a mighty wrench, the house left the ground and swung high in the air.

It turned three times on its cable. Then it became a house on wheels.

"I shall call our house 'Spirit of Hope'," shouted Dad, and he dipped his brush into a can of black paint.

The Fairweathers' house bumped along the road all the way to the docks.

Now, even on the darkest night, there is a light glowing
at the end of the pier. The house seems to be pulling
gently at its moorings, wanting to slip away with the tide.

"Who will be Captain tonight?" ask Cecily, Lilly, Micky, Duggy, and Sammy.

"Mary," says Dad.